C0-FNX-477

Old MacDonald Had a Farm

and other favorite children's songs

Illustrated by
Hannah Wood

tiger tales®

Old MacDonald Had a Farm

Old MacDonald had a farm, E-I-E-I-O!
And on this farm he had some cows, E-I-E-I-O!
With a moo, moo here, and a moo, moo there,
Here a moo, there a moo, everywhere a moo, moo.
Old MacDonald had a farm, E-I-E-I-O!

Old MacDonald had a farm, E-I-E-I-O!
And on this farm he had some pigs, E-I-E-I-O!
With an oink, oink here, and an oink, oink there,
Here an oink, there an oink, everywhere an oink, oink.
Old MacDonald had a farm, E-I-E-I-O!

Good Morning to You

Good morning to you,
Good morning to you,
Good morning, dear baby,
Good morning to you!

Mr. Sun

Oh, Mr. Sun, Sun, Mr. Golden Sun,
Please shine down on me.
Oh, Mr. Sun, Sun, Mr. Golden Sun,
Hiding behind a tree.
These little children are asking you
To please come out so
We can play with you.

Oh, Mr. Sun, Sun, Mr. Golden Sun,
Please shine down on,
Please shine down on,
Please shine down on me!

Here We Go Round the Mulberry Bush

Here we go 'round the mulberry bush,
The mulberry bush, the mulberry bush.
Here we go 'round the mulberry bush,
So early in the morning.

This is the way we brush our teeth,
Brush our teeth, brush our teeth.
This is the way we brush our teeth,
So early in the morning.

This is the way we wash our face,
Wash our face, wash our face.
This is the way we wash our face,
So early in the morning.

This is the way we comb our hair,
Comb our hair, comb our hair.
This is the way we comb our hair,
So early in the morning.

Skip to My Lou

Skip, skip, skip to my Lou,
Skip, skip, skip to my Lou,
Skip, skip, skip to my Lou,
Skip to my Lou, my darlin'!

Fly's in the buttermilk,
Shoo, fly, shoo,
Fly's in the buttermilk,
Shoo, fly, shoo,
Fly's in the buttermilk,
Shoo, fly, shoo,
Skip to my Lou, my darlin'!

I'm a Little Teapot

I'm a little teapot, short and stout,
Here is my handle, here is my spout.
When I get all steamed up, hear me shout,
"Tip me over and pour me out!"

Do Your Ears Hang Low?

Do your ears hang low?
Do they wobble to and fro?
Can you tie them in a knot?
Can you tie them in a bow?
Can you fling them over your shoulder
Like a Continental soldier?
Do your ears hang low?

The Farmer in the Dell

The farmer in the dell,
The farmer in the dell,
Heigh ho, the derry-o!
The farmer in the dell.

The farmer takes a wife,
The farmer takes a wife,
Heigh ho, the derry-o!
The farmer takes a wife.

The wife takes a child . . .

The child takes a cat . . .

The cat takes a rat . . .

The rat takes the cheese . . .

The cheese stands alone . . .

Pop! Goes the Weasel

All around the mulberry bush,
The monkey chased the weasel.
The monkey thought 'twas all in fun,
Pop! goes the weasel.

A-Tisket, A-Tasket

A-tisket, a-tasket,
A green and yellow basket,
I wrote a letter to my friend,
And on the way I dropped it.
I dropped it,
I dropped it,
And on the way I dropped it.
A little boy picked it up
And put it in his pocket.

The Bear Went Over the Mountain

The bear went over the mountain,
The bear went over the mountain,
The bear went over the mountain
To see what he could see.

To see what he could see,
To see what he could see.

The other side of the mountain,
The other side of the mountain,
The other side of the mountain
Was all that he could see!

Bingo

There was a farmer had a dog,
And Bingo was his name, O!

B-I-N-G-O!

B-I-N-G-O!

B-I-N-G-O!

And Bingo was his name, O!